Library of Congress Cataloging-in-Publication Data
Stojic, Manya.
Wet pebbles under our feet / by Manya Stojic.
p.   cm.
Summary: A visit to Grandpa and Grandma on their pebbly island brings alive old family stories.
ISBN 0-375-81519-8 (trade) — ISBN 0-375-91519-2 (lib. bdg.)
[1. Grandfathers—Fiction. 2. Grandmothers—Fiction. 3. Family life—Fiction. 4. Islands—Fiction.] I. Title.
PZ7.S873 We 2002
[E]—dc21   2001038137
Printed in China
April 2002
10 9 8 7 6 5 4 3 2 1
First American Edition

To my mum Ruža and my uncle Raša who taught me to love the sea.
M.S.

Wet
Pebbles
under
our feet

Wet
Pebbles
under
our feet

Manya Stojic

Alfred A. Knopf  New York

Whenever we go to the sea, my mum tells me stories that always start the same way.

Far away in the deep blue sea is a small island with a pebbly shore. A **fisherman** lives there with his **wife** and their three children, **Marco, Mara,** and **Mario.**

Mara is my mum's name.
And the stories she tells
are about **her** family
growing up on that island . . .

far away,
in the deep blue sea.

The fisherman and his wife are my **grandpa** and **grandma**.

We are on our way to see them.

Me, my mum, my uncle Marco,
and my uncle Mario.

"I remember how **blue** the water was," says Uncle Marco. "And playing **pirates.** Papa used to get **SO** mad when we played with his fishing bucket."

"I remember **running** for the **ferry** to **school**," says Uncle Mario, "and **always** being late because of **you**, Marco!"

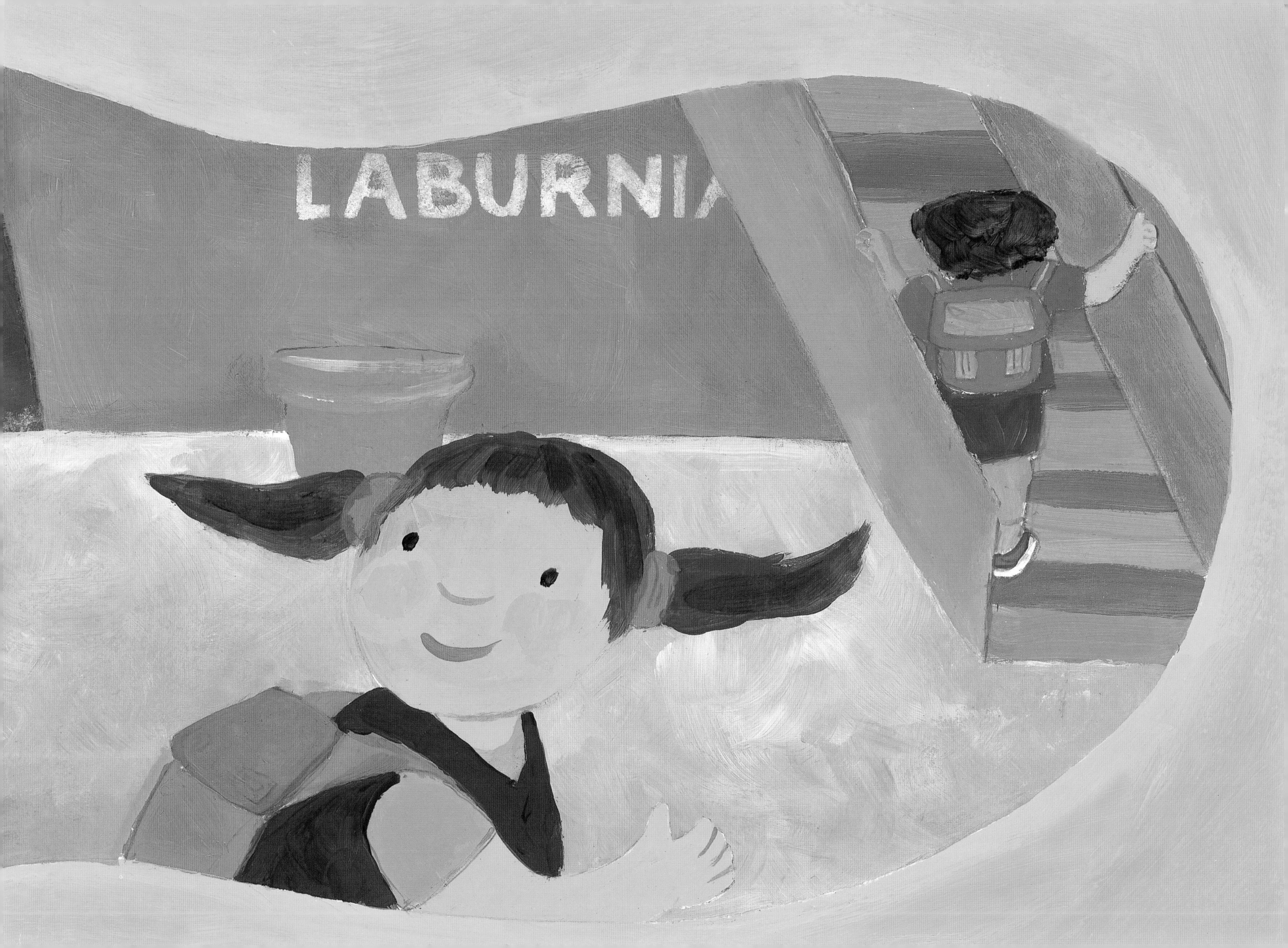
LABURNIA

“And fresh fish soup.

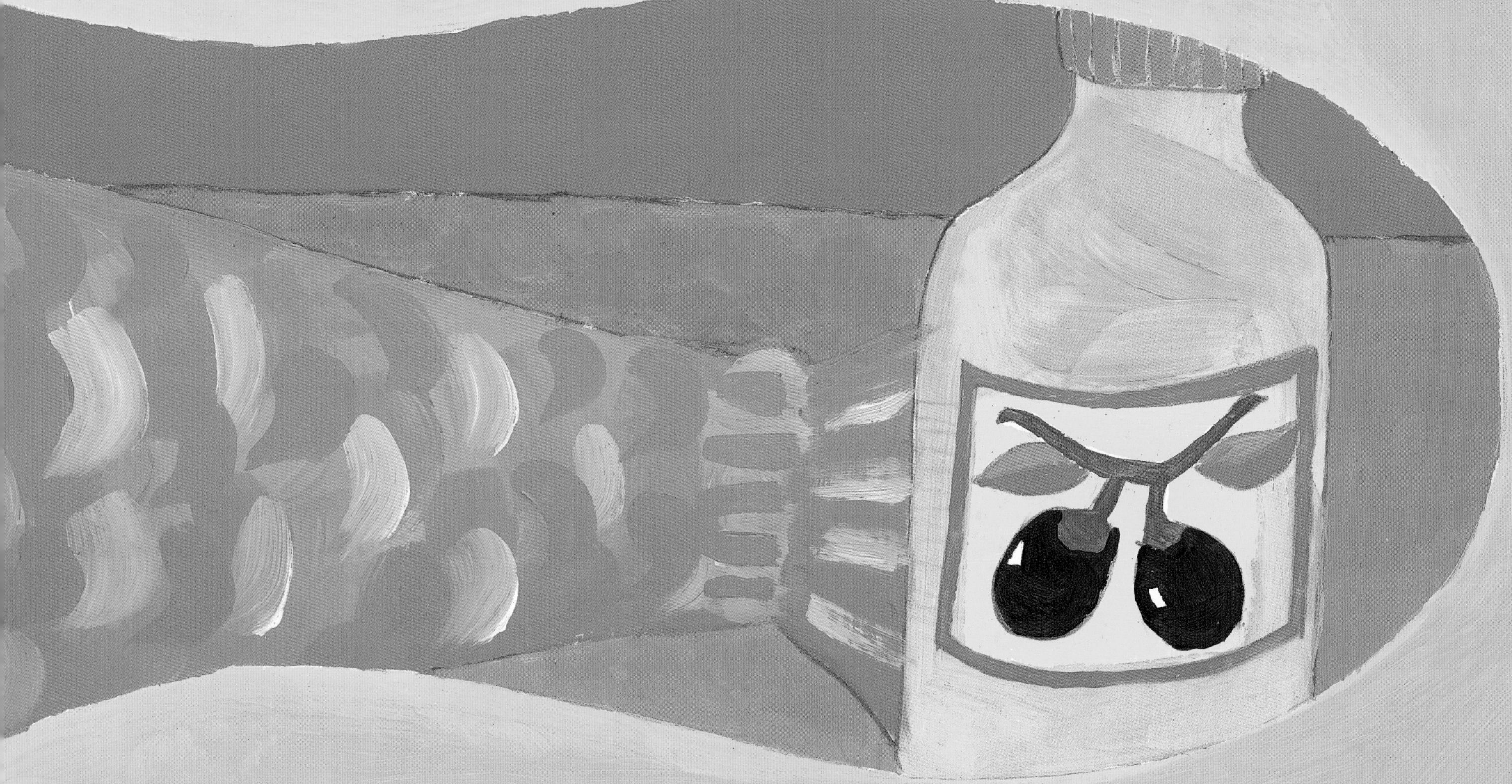

You could **smell** it from far away.”

"I still **love** that taste," says Uncle Marco.

"I still hate that **smell!**" says Uncle Mario.

And we all laugh.

"Tell me more," I say.
"Tell me about the pebbles."

"**Ah, yes,**" they sigh. "**There's nothing like the feel of wet pebbles under your feet. Wet and cool and smooth.**"

I look out over the **clear blue sea** and **there** is our **tiny** island **glittering** in the distance.

Soon we are there.
Grandpa and **Grandma**
are **waving** from the shore.

"Grandma! We're here!"

"Welcome **home**, sweetie."

"Come on," says Grandma, "the fish soup is waiting . . ."

I take off my shoes
and walk along
the beach,
feeling those
wet pebbles
under my feet . . .

. . . and I have a new story— about a **fisherman,** his **wife,** their three **children** . . . and their **granddaughter.**